Disney's
THE
LION KING

RAVETTE PUBLISHING

First published by Ravette Books Ltd 1994
Reprinted by Ravette Publishing Ltd 1995

Printed and bound for Ravette Publishing Ltd,
Unit 3, Tristar Centre,
Star Road, Partridge Green,
West Sussex RH13 8RA

by BPC Paulton Books Ltd, Bristol

ISBN: 1 853386 333 5

A NEW DAWN IN AFRICA . . .

. . . ANOTHER DAY TO SEE, TO HEAR, TO SMELL, TO DO . . .

. . . TO LIVE!

LIFE HOLDS SO *MUCH*, AND TIME SEEMS SO *SHORT* . . .

. . . BUT EVEN AS THE GREAT CIRCLE OF THE *SUN* BEGINS ANEW ITS JOURNEY ACROSS THE ENDLESS SKIES . . .

. . . SO ON THIS MORNING DOES A *NEW LIFE* BEGIN ITS JOURNEY . . .

. . . THE JOURNEY CALLED *LIVING* . . .

. . . AND A SEARCH FOR A PLACE IN THE GREAT *CIRCLE OF LIFE!*

LATER, AND ELSEWHERE...

squeek!

FWAP!

LIFE'S NOT FAIR. YOU SEE, I SHALL NEVER BE **KING**—AND **YOU** SHALL NEVER SEE ANOTHER **DAY.**

GOODBYE.

SQUEEK!

DIDN'T YOUR MOTHER EVER TELL YOU NOT TO **PLAY** WITH YOUR **FOOD?**

ZAZU! YOU MADE ME LOSE MY LUNCH!

I'M HERE TO ANNOUNCE THAT **KING MUFASA'S** ON HIS WAY! AND YOU'D BETTER HAVE A **GOOD EXCUSE** FOR MISSING THE **CEREMONY** THIS MORNING!

HELP-!!

SNAP!

SCAR! **DROP** HIM!

PTUI!

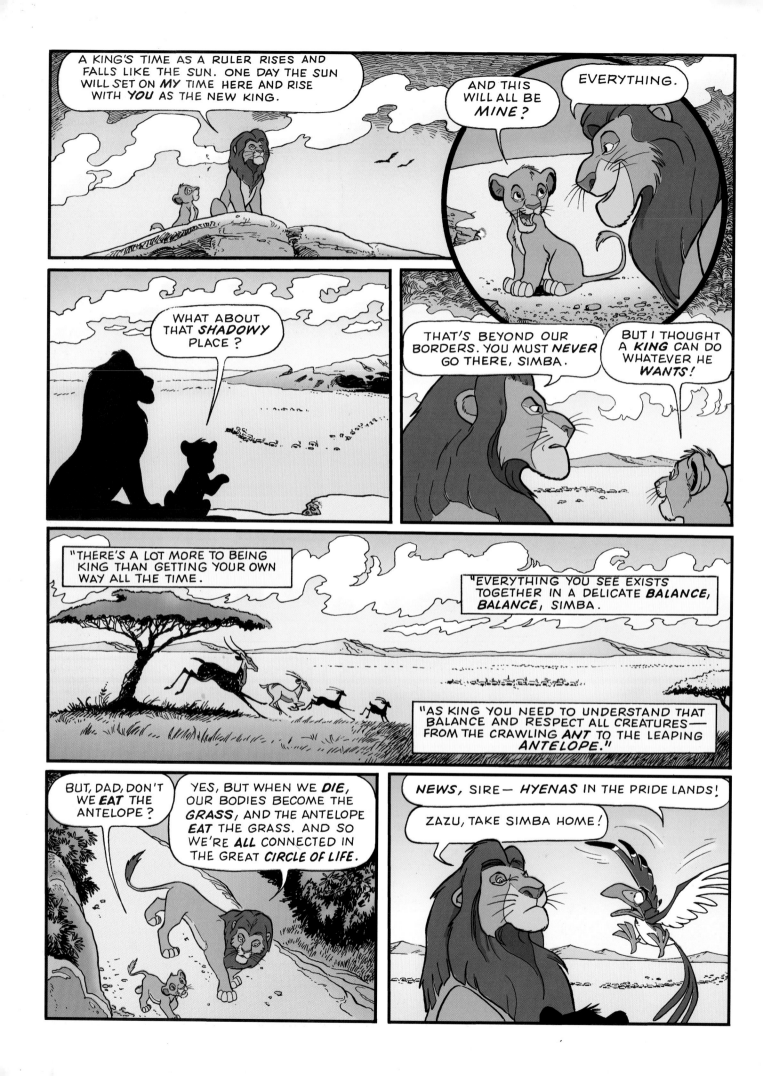

AND WHILE MUFASA GOES TO INVESTIGATE . . .

HEY, UNCLE SCAR, GUESS WHAT? I'M GONNA BE *KING* OF PRIDE ROCK!

FORGIVE ME FOR NOT LEAPING FOR JOY. *BAD BACK,* YOU KNOW.

SO YOUR FATHER SHOWED YOU THE WHOLE KINGDOM, DID HE? HE DIDN'T SHOW YOU WHAT'S BEYOND THAT RISE AT THE NORTHERN BORDER . . .

WELL, NO . . . HE SAID I MUSTN'T *GO* THERE!

AND HE'S ABSOLUTELY *RIGHT.* ONLY THE BRAVEST OF LIONS GO THERE.

WELL, *I'M* BRAVE! WHAT'S OUT THERE?

I CAN'T TELL YOU.

WHY NOT?

SIMBA, SIMBA . . . I'M ONLY LOOKING OUT FOR THE WELL-BEING OF MY FAVOURITE NEPHEW. AN *ELEPHANT GRAVEYARD* IS NO PLACE FOR—

AN ELEPHANT *WHAT?!*

OOPS— I'VE SAID TOO MUCH. I SUPPOSE YOU'D HAVE FOUND OUT SOONER OR LATER, YOU BEING SO CLEVER AND ALL.

PROMISE ME YOU'LL *NEVER* VISIT THAT DREADFUL PLACE.

NO PROBLEM!

THERE'S A GOOD LAD. IT'LL BE OUR LITTLE *SECRET!*

OH... RIGHT! HOW'RE WE GONNA *DITCH* THE *DODO*?

JUST LOOK AT YOU TWO — LITTLE SEEDS OF *ROMANCE* BLOSSOMING IN THE SAVANNAH! YOUR PARENTS WILL BE THRILLED, WHAT WITH YOU BEING *BETROTHED* AND ALL!

BE-*WHAT*??

YOU AND NALA ARE *BETROTHED!* ONE DAY YOU TWO ARE GOING TO BE *MARRIED!*

I'M GONNA MARRY *HER*?!

Yuuuuck!

Eeeuwww!!

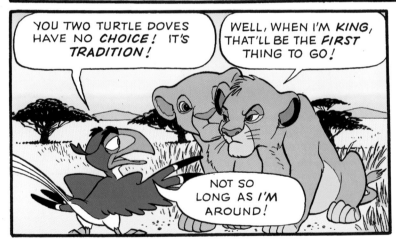

YOU TWO TURTLE DOVES HAVE NO *CHOICE!* IT'S *TRADITION!*

WELL, WHEN I'M *KING,* THAT'LL BE THE *FIRST* THING TO GO!

NOT SO LONG AS *I'M* AROUND!

IN THAT CASE, YOU'RE *FIRED!*

NICE *TRY,* BUT ONLY THE *KING* CAN DO THAT!

WELL, HE'S THE *FUTURE* KING!

SO YOU *HAVE* TO DO WHAT I *TELL* YOU!

NOT YET I DON'T! AND WITH AN ATTITUDE LIKE *THAT,* I'M AFRAID YOU'LL BE A PRETTY *PATHETIC* KING, INDEED!

NOT THE WAY *I* SEE IT!

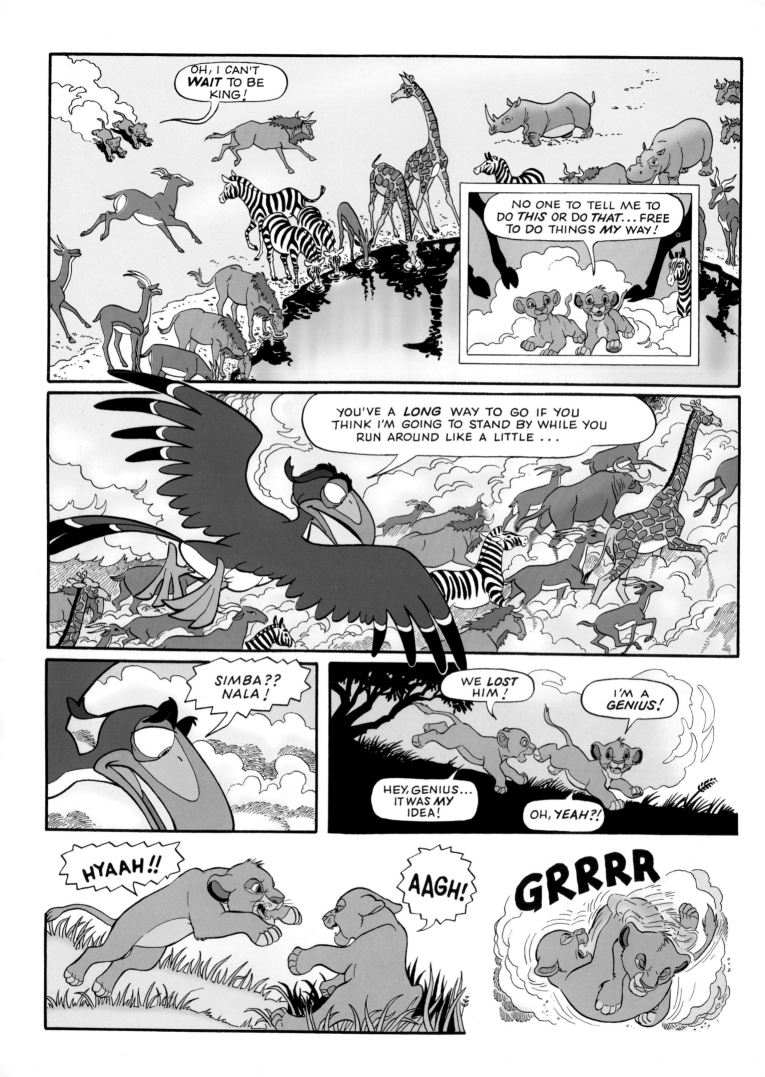

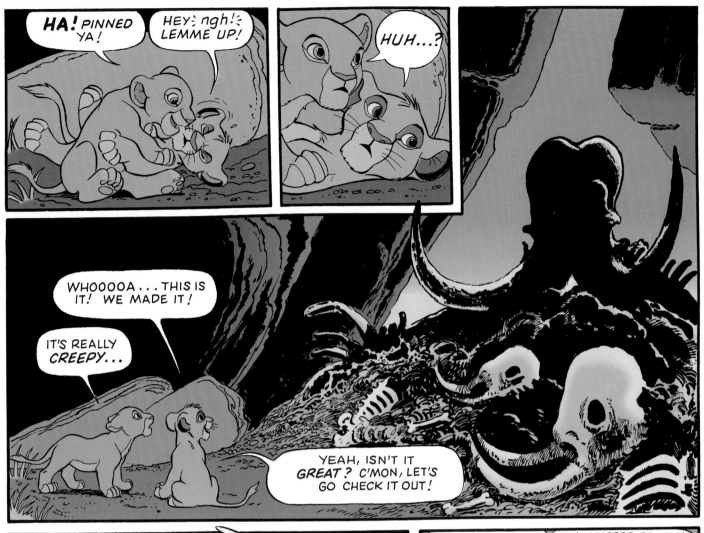

HEE HEE HEE

HEE HEE HEE

WELL, WELL, WELL, BANZAI... WHAT HAVE WE GOT *HERE*?

HMM... I DON'T KNOW, SHENZI! WHAT DO YOU THINK, ED?

JUST WHAT I WAS THINKIN'— A TRIO OF *TRESPASSERS!*

AND QUITE BY *ACCIDENT*, LET ME ASSURE YOU! I AM THE KING'S *MAJORDOMO!*

AND THAT WOULD MAKE *YOU*—

THE *FUTURE KING!*

OOO! WELL, I THINK YOUR FUTURE JUST *RAN OUT!*

PAH! YOU CAN'T DO ANYTHING TO ME!

HEE HEE HEE

ER... TECHNICALLY, THEY *CAN*. WE ARE ON *THEIR* LAND.

BUT *THEY* SNEAK ONTO *OUR* LAND ALL THE TIME!

ZAZU'S TOLD ME ABOUT YOU! HE SAYS YOU'RE NOTHING BUT *SLOBBERING, MANGY, STUPID—*

...POACHERS!

IX-NAY ON THE *OOPID-STAY!*

HEY! WHO YOU CALLIN' *"OOPID-STAY"?!*

OH, MY-MY-MY, LOOK AT THE *SUN!* TIME TO *GO!*

WHAT'S THE HURRY? WE'D *LOVE* YOU TO STICK AROUND FOR *DINNER!*

YEAH! WE COULD HAVE WHATEVER'S *"LION"* AROUND! GET IT? *"LION"* AROUND?!

HEE HEE HEE

OH MAN! I CAN'T REMEMBER THE LAST TIME I HAD *LION CUBS* FOR DINNER!

HEY!

WAIT- WAIT- WAIT! *I'M* HAVING THE LION CUBS!

YOU WILL *NOT!* YOU CAN HAVE THE *BIRD!*

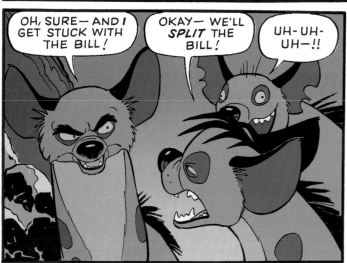

FWAP!

OOCH, OWW—!

HEY, STOPPIT!

SILENCE! IF YOU EVER COME NEAR MY SON AGAIN...

SON? THIS IS YOUR SON?! OH MAN, WE DIDN'T KNOW! DID YOU KNOW, BANZAI?

ME? NO! DID YOU?

NO, OF COURSE NOT!

DID YOU KNOW, ED?

RATTLE!

RATTLE!

RATTLE!

ROOOARR!!

TOOTLES!

DAD, I'M... I'M SORRY.

LET'S GO HOME.

ZAZU, TAKE NALA HOME. I HAVE TO TEACH MY SON A LESSON.

VERY GOOD, SIRE...

SOON, UNDER THE FIRE OF THE SETTING SUN . . .

SIMBA, I'M VERY *DISAPPOINTED* IN YOU.

I KNOW . . .

YOU COULD HAVE BEEN *KILLED!* YOU DELIBERATELY DISOBEYED ME! AND WHAT'S WORSE, YOU PUT *NALA* IN DANGER!

I WAS JUST TRYING TO BE *BRAVE,* LIKE YOU!

I'M ONLY BRAVE WHEN I *HAVE* TO BE, SIMBA . . . BEING BRAVE DOESN'T MEAN YOU GO *LOOKING* FOR TROUBLE.

BUT *YOU'RE* NOT SCARED OF ANYTHING!

I WAS TODAY.

YOU *WERE??*

YES. I THOUGHT I MIGHT LOSE YOU.

OH. I GUESS EVEN KINGS GET SCARED, HUH?

C'MERE, YOU.

grrrr!

HEE HEE!

YOU'RE GREAT, SIMBA.

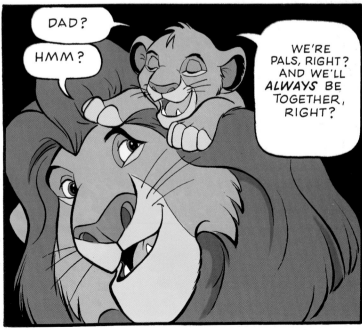

DAD?

HMM?

WE'RE PALS, RIGHT? AND WE'LL *ALWAYS* BE TOGETHER, RIGHT?

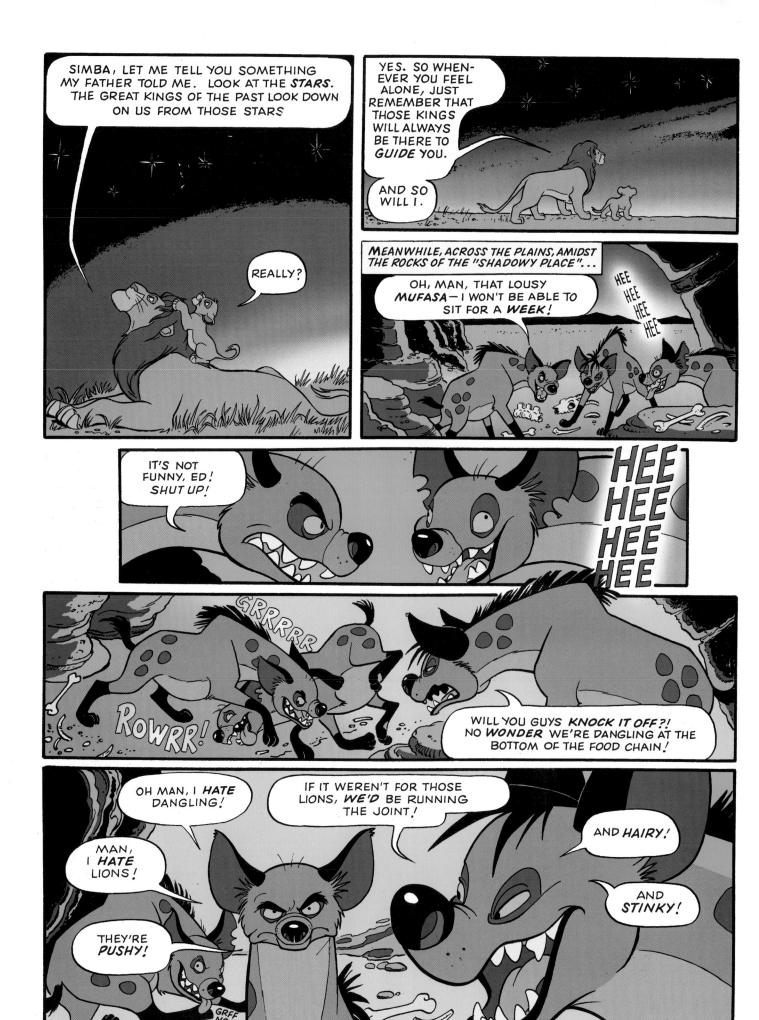

THE NEXT DAY...

WAIT HERE. YOUR FATHER HAS A MARVELLOUS *SURPRISE* FOR YOU.

WHAT IS IT?

IF I TOLD YOU, IT WOULDN'T BE A SURPRISE, NOW WOULD IT?

IF YOU TELL ME, I'LL STILL ACT SURPRISED!

⸝ TSK TSK ⸝ YOU ARE SUCH A NAUGHTY BOY. NO, THIS IS JUST FOR YOU AND YOUR DAD. YOU KNOW, A SORT OF FATHER-SON ... THING.

WELL, I'D BETTER GO GET HIM.

I'LL GO WITH YOU!

NO, NO — JUST STAY ON THIS ROCK. YOU WOULDN'T WANT TO END UP IN ANOTHER MESS LIKE YOU DID WITH THE HYENAS.

YOU *KNOW* ABOUT THAT?

SIMBA, *EVERYONE* KNOWS ABOUT THAT.

REALLY...?

YOU'RE LUCKY "DADDY" WAS THERE TO SAVE YOU. OH, AND JUST BETWEEN US... YOU MIGHT LIKE TO WORK ON THAT LITTLE ROAR OF YOURS.

OH. OKAY.

HEY, UNCLE SCAR ... WILL I LIKE THE SURPRISE?

SIMBA, IT'S TO DIE FOR.

RRRRUMBLE! RRRUMBLE!

GASP!

THE HERD MOVES LIKE A GREAT BLACK FLOOD...

...AND THE EARTH TREMBLES WITH THE POUNDING OF A THOUSAND HOOVES!

BUT THE WILDEBEEST DO NOT MOVE OF THEIR OWN ACCORD...

AND CLOSE BY...

LOOK, SIRE! THE HERD IS ON THE MOVE!

ODD...

SCAR, THIS IS AWFUL! I'LL GO BACK FOR HELP!

GRRRR!

FWAK!

BOMP!

CRASH!

YIIEEEEEE-!!

UHH-!

DAD!!!

THE HERD MOVES LIKE A GREAT BLACK FLOOD...

... AND THE EARTH TREMBLES WITH THE POUNDING OF A THOUSAND HOOVES...

SCAR, HELP ME! BROTHER...
... HELP ME?!

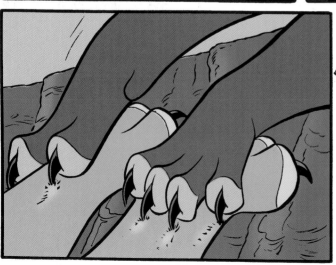

LONG LIVE THE KING!

NOOOOOO !!!

DAD!!

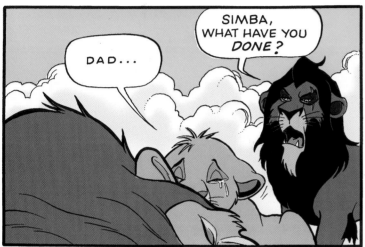

DAD...

SIMBA, WHAT HAVE YOU *DONE*?

THERE...THERE WERE WILDEBEESTS... HE...HE TRIED TO SAVE ME...IT WAS AN *ACCIDENT*...I DIDN'T MEAN FOR IT TO...

OF COURSE YOU DIDN'T. NO ONE EVER *MEANS* FOR THESE THINGS TO HAPPEN.

BUT THE KING IS *DEAD*. IF IT WEREN'T FOR *YOU*, HE'D STILL BE *ALIVE*.

OH, WHAT WILL YOUR *MOTHER* THINK?

WH...WHAT AM I GONNA *DO*...?

RUN AWAY, SIMBA. *RUN*. RUN AWAY AND *NEVER RETURN!*

KILL HIM!

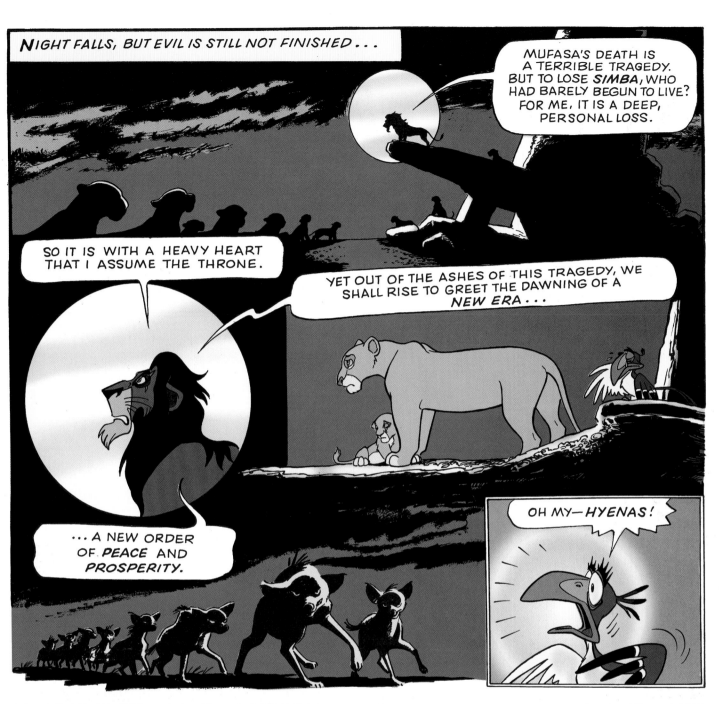

NIGHT FALLS, BUT EVIL IS STILL NOT FINISHED...

MUFASA'S DEATH IS A TERRIBLE TRAGEDY. BUT TO LOSE *SIMBA*, WHO HAD BARELY BEGUN TO LIVE? FOR ME, IT IS A DEEP, PERSONAL LOSS.

SO IT IS WITH A HEAVY HEART THAT I ASSUME THE THRONE.

YET OUT OF THE ASHES OF THIS TRAGEDY, WE SHALL RISE TO GREET THE DAWNING OF A *NEW ERA*...

...A NEW ORDER OF *PEACE* AND *PROSPERITY*.

OH MY— HYENAS!

SCAR, DO SOMETHING!

A NEW ORDER OF PEACE AND PROSPERITY IN WHICH *LION* AND *HYENA* COME TOGETHER IN A GREAT AND GLORIOUS FUTURE!

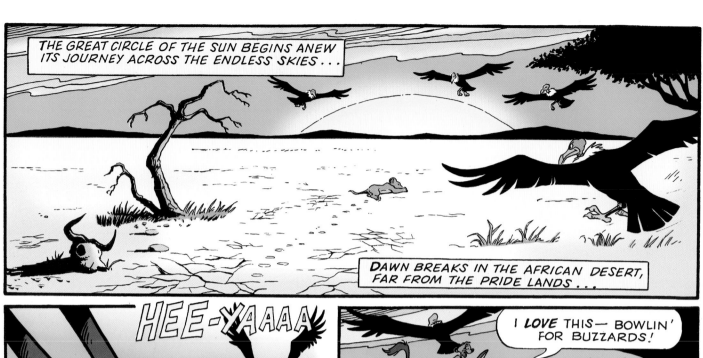

THE GREAT CIRCLE OF THE SUN BEGINS ANEW ITS JOURNEY ACROSS THE ENDLESS SKIES...

DAWN BREAKS IN THE AFRICAN DESERT, FAR FROM THE PRIDE LANDS...

HEE-YAAAA

I *LOVE* THIS— BOWLIN' FOR BUZZARDS!

UH-OH. HEY, TIMON, YA BETTER COME LOOK! I THINK IT'S STILL *ALIVE!*

ACK-ACK-ACK!

HEYY, IT'S A *LION!* RUN, PUMBAA! MOVE IT!

AW, TIMON, IT'S JUST A *LITTLE* LION. LOOK AT HIM—HE'S SO CUTE AND ALL ALONE.

CAN WE KEEP HIM?

PUMBAA, ARE YOU *NUTS?!* YOU'RE TALKING ABOUT A *LION!* LIONS *EAT* GUYS LIKE US!

BUT HE'S SO *LITTLE.*

HE'S GONNA GET *BIGGER!*

MAYBE HE'LL BE ON *OUR* SIDE.

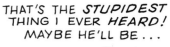

THAT'S THE *STUPIDEST* THING I EVER *HEARD!* MAYBE HE'LL BE...

HEY! I GOT IT! WHAT IF HE'S ON OUR SIDE?! Y'KNOW, HAVIN' A LION AROUND MIGHT NOT BE SUCH A BAD IDEA!

SO WE'RE *KEEPIN'* HIM?

pfft! OF COURSE WE'RE KEEPIN' HIM! WHO'S THE BRAINS OF THIS OUTFIT?

UHHH..

MY POINT EXACTLY!

*A*ND SOON, AT THE EDGE OF THE JUNGLE...

YOU OKAY, KID?

I... GUESS SO.

YOU NEARLY DIED! I SAVED YOU!

WELL, PUMBAA HELPED. A LITTLE.

THANKS.

HEY, WHERE YA GOIN'?

NOWHERE.

WELL, WHERE'RE YA FROM?

WHO CARES? I CAN'T GO BACK.

AH, YOU'RE AN OUTCAST! THAT'S GREAT! SO ARE WE!

HEY, WHAD'JA DO, KID?

IF I TOLD YOU, YOU'D HATE ME.

ANYTHING WE CAN DO?

Y'KNOW, KID, IN TIMES LIKE THIS MY BUDDY TIMON HERE SAYS: "YOU GOTTA PUT YOUR BEHIND IN YOUR PAST!"

NO-NO-NO! AMATEUR! IT'S: "YOU GOTTA PUT YOUR PAST BEHIND YOU"

LOOK, KID, BAD THINGS HAPPEN, AND YOU CAN'T DO ANYTHING ABOUT IT, RIGHT?

RIGHT.

WRONG! WHEN THE WORLD TURNS ITS BACK ON YOU, YOU TURN YOUR BACK ON THE WORLD! REPEAT AFTER ME: HAKUNA MATATA!

WHAT?

HA-KU-NA MA-TA-TA. IT MEANS "NO WORRIES."

TWO LITTLE WORDS THAT'LL CHANGE YOUR LIFE. KID, I WASN'T ALWAYS THE CALM, COOL MEERCAT YOU SEE BEFORE YOU, NO SIREE! WHY...

...WHEN I WAS YOUNG, I LIVED IN THE MEERCAT COLONY, ACCEPTING WITHOUT QUESTION THE PREVAILING VIEW THAT LIFE WAS ONE LONG UPHILL CLIMB!

I DID AS I WAS TOLD, DUG HOLES, STOOD GUARD, TILL ONE DAY IT CROSSED MY MIND...

...THAT I WAS WRONG AND THAT ALL I NEEDED TO DO WAS HEED...

HAKUNA MATATA

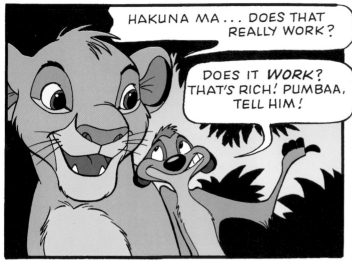

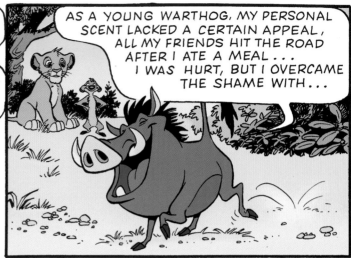

SIGH
HAKUNA MATATA...

SPOP!

SIMBA! IT IS TIME...

MEANWHILE, TIME IN THE JUNGLE FOLLOWS ITS OWN RHYTHM..

♫ HUSH, HUSH, MY LITTLE ONE, THE LION SLEEPS IN THE JUNGLE TONIGHT! ♫

OH-VOH-DEE-OH-DOH!

WELL, NOW— WHAT HAVE WE HERE?

YIPE!

GRRRRR!

SQEEEAL!

ROOOOARR!

IT'S ME — SIMBA!

SIMBA...??

IT'S GREAT TO SEE YA, NALA!

AND IT'S GREAT TO SEE YOU, TOO! WHAT ARE YOU DOING HERE?

I LIVE HERE!

COULD YOU GUYS EXCUSE US FOR A FEW MINUTES?

MAYBE YOU BETTER GO.

YA THINK YA KNOW A GUY...

NALA, WHAT IS IT?

IT'S LIKE YOU'RE BACK FROM THE DEAD. YOU DON'T KNOW HOW MUCH THIS COULD *MEAN* TO EVERYONE... WHAT IT MEANS TO *ME*...

I'VE REALLY *MISSED* YOU.

I'VE MISSED YOU, TOO.

I TELL YA, PUMBAA. THIS *STINKS*.

OH. SORRY.

NOT YOU— *THEM!*

HIM... HER.....*ALOOONE!*

DON'TCHA *FEEL* IT? THE SIGNS OF *LOVE* ARE THERE...

...MOONLIGHT, FIREFLIES...

...DISASTER IN THE AIR! IF HE FALLS FOR HER, OUR PAL IS *DOOMED!*

WAAAAAOOO..!!

BUT NIGHT FALLS WITHOUT ANOTHER WORD, AND A YOUNG KING SITS ALONE UNDER THE STARS . . .

YOU TOLD ME YOU'D ALWAYS BE THERE FOR ME— BUT YOU'RE NOT. IT'S BECAUSE OF ME. IT'S MY FAULT. *IT'S ALL MY FAULT*...

SIMBA WANDERS THE JUNGLE IN DESPAIR, BUT HE IS NOT ALONE. A HAUNTING VOICE FOLLOWS IN THE DARKNESS . . .

♪ ASANTE SANA. SQUASH BANANA. WE WE NUGU. MI MI APANA ♪

FINALLY...

WILL YA CUT IT OUT?!

CAN'T CUT IT OUT. IT'LL GROW RIGHT BACK!

WHO ARE YOU?

THE QUESTION IS, WHO ARE YOU?

I THOUGHT I KNEW. NOW I'M NOT SO SURE.

I KNOW WHO YOU ARE. YOU'RE *MUFASA'S* BOY!

YOU KNEW MY FATHER?

CORRECTION. I *KNOW* YOUR FATHER.

MY FATHER DIED A LONG TIME AGO.

WRONG AGAIN! HE'S ALIVE! OLD RAFIKI WILL SHOW HIM TO YOU!

LOOK DOWN THERE!

THAT'S JUST MY *REFLECTION*!

NO, LOOK *HARDER*!

MAYBE IT'S TIME TO START.

THEN WHAT ARE YOU *WAITING* FOR? GO ON! HURRY UP! *SCAT!* DON'T DAWDLE!

LATER THAT NIGHT...

HAVE YOU GUYS SEEN SIMBA?

I THOUGHT HE WAS WITH YOU!

YOU WON'T FIND HIM HERE! THE KING HAS *RETURNED!*

HE'S REALLY GONE BACK?

WHAT DO YOU MEAN?

SIMBA'S GONE BACK TO CHALLENGE HIS UNCLE TO TAKE HIS PLACE AS KING!

OHHHH...

MUCH LATER AND FAR AWAY, THE ONE TRUE KING SURVEYS HIS KINGDOM...

SIMBA, YOU FORGOT TO SAY GOODBYE.

I FORGOT TO SAY A *LOT* OF THINGS. AFTER LAST NIGHT, I THOUGHT I'D NEVER *SEE* YOU AGAIN.

SIMBA, WHATEVER I *SAID* ... IT'S BECAUSE I *CARE* ABOUT YOU.

NO—I NEEDED TO HEAR IT.

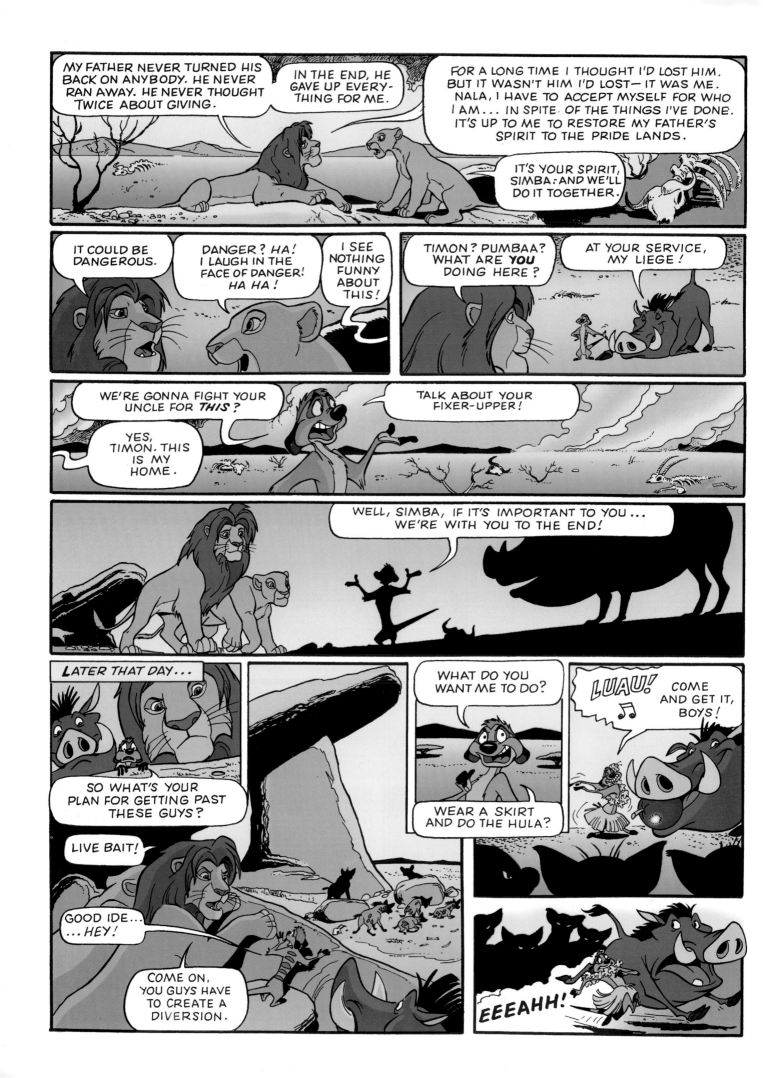

AAAAAHH-!!

NOW *THIS* LOOKS FAMILIAR! WHERE HAVE I SEEN THIS *BEFORE?* LET *ME* THINK... AH, YES—I REMEMBER! THAT'S JUST THE WAY YOUR *FATHER* LOOKED BEFORE HE *DIED!*

JUST ONE THING BEFORE YOU GO...

...I *KILLED* HIM!

ROARRR!

HELP ME, YOU IDIOTS!

ROOOAR!

THE HYENAS, SOUNDLY BEATEN, RETREAT TO SEEK THEIR REVENGE...

HEE-YAAAAH!